GATEWAY TO IMAGINATION®

A Book Club *from* Discovery Toys

Open a book and unlock your
gateway to imagination

From the Library of

_____

Cadillac

by **Charles Temple**

illustrated by **Lynne Lockhart**

G. P. Putnam's Sons   New York

Text copyright © 1995 by Charles Temple
Illustrations copyright © 1995 by Lynne Lockhart
G. P. Putnam's Sons, a division of The Putnam & Grosset Group, 200 Madison Avenue,
New York, NY 10016. G. P. Putnam's Sons, Reg. U.S. Pat. & Tm. Off.
Published simultaneously in Canada.
Printed in Hong Kong.
Type designed by Patrick Collins. Text set in Calisto.

Library of Congress Cataloging in Publication Data
Temple, Charles A., 1947-   Cadillac / by Charles Temple;
illustrated by Lynne Lockhart.   p.   cm.
Summary: A rhyming story that describes the excitement of going for a ride with Granny
in her old Cadillac, as she "cruises through traffic like a bull through a dance."
[1. Grandmothers—Fiction.   2. Automobile driving—Fiction.   3. Stories in rhyme.]
1. Lockhart, Lynne N., ill.   II. Title.   PZ8.3.T2187Cad   1995   [E]—dc20   93-42387 CIP AC
ISBN 0-399-22654-0

3   5   7   9   10   8   6   4

Cadillac is a trademark of General Motors

BOOM, SHACKA-LACKA-LACKA,
BOOM, SHACKA-LACK.
When my granny starts up her old Cadillac
With the Naugahyde seats
And the gold-flecked metal,
You can hear seven cylinders talking right back
When she stomps her little foot
On the big gas pedal.
Then the valves start clattering, tacka-tack-tack,
When my granny starts up her old Cadillac.
BOOM, SHACKA-LACKA-LACKA,
BOOM, SHACKA-LACK.

Granny drops it in reverse and the Cadillac rocks
And it roars and it rumbles
Like a pent-up lion.
Now we're out of the garage like a jack-in-the-box.
We may be going backwards,
But we're already flyin'.

Better jump for your life, and never look back
When my granny takes a ride in her old Cadillac.
BOOM, SHACKA-LACKA-LACKA,
BOOM, SHACKA-LACK.

Granny sweeps like a duchess down the middle of the street,
With her long tail-fins
And her wire wheel-covers.
I'm scrunched down small in the big back seat.
I've remembered two prayers
And I'm thinking up others.

It's amazing how my sweet mama's teachings come back
When I'm riding with my granny in her old Cadillac.
BOOM, SHACKA-LACKA-LACKA,
BOOM, SHACKA-LACK.

Granny cruises through the traffic like a bull through a dance.
To the left and the right,
Cars are heading for the shoulder.
And the little foreign numbers never really have a chance,
But the trucks and the buses
Act a whole lot bolder.

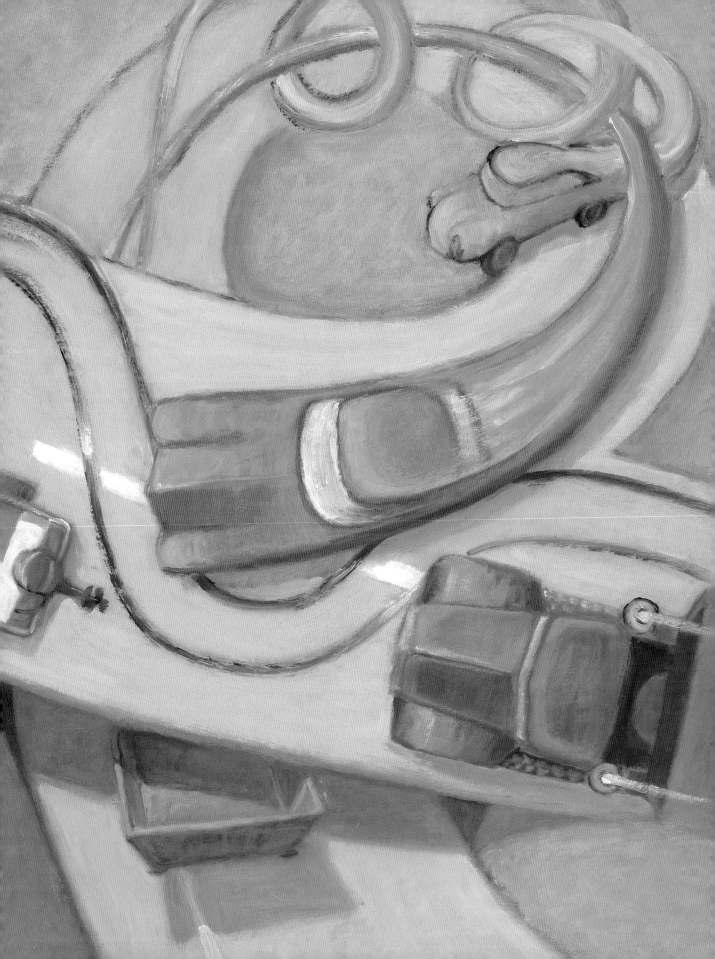

"They're honking at us, Granny." Granny waves right back.
"Folks surely do admire this old Cadillac."
BOOM, SHACKA-LACKA-LACKA,
BOOM, SHACKA-LACK.

Granny can't tell color since the day she was born—
Not her yellow from her green,
Nor her green from her red.
When she gets to a corner she just lays on her horn.
This makes the other cars
And the trucks stop dead.

What bellows like a moose or a lovesick yak?
It's my granny coming through in her old Cadillac.
BOOM, SHACKA-LACKA-LACKA,
BOOM, SHACKA-LACK.

We arrive downtown and the Cadillac stops
And the cars start honking,
And the dogs start barking.
'Cause the traffic stands still while my grandmama shops.
"Aren't we blocking up the street
By the way we're parking?"

Folks shout, folks fuss, folks yacky-yack-yack.
"Folks *do* carry on about that old Cadillac."
BOOM, SHACKA-LACKA-LACKA,
BOOM, SHACKA-LACK.

A man in blue with a big black pen
And a pad full of tickets
Is a-frowning at the car.
Then my granny shuffles up with a great big grin:
"Were you writing us a note?
What a sweetie you are!"

She kisses his cheek and she pats his back
And we leave him staring at her old Cadillac.
BOOM, SHACKA-LACKA-LACKA,
BOOM, SHACKA-LACK.

"Home again," says Granny. "We're safe and sound."
  And my knees are knocking
  And my teeth are grinding.
  I hug my granny, then I kiss the ground,
  And I count my body parts
'Cause I need some reminding
  That all of us went, and all of us came back
  From a ride with my granny in her old Cadillac.

BOOM, SHACKA-LACKA-LACKA,
BOOM, SHACKA-LACK.